Beauty SPOT

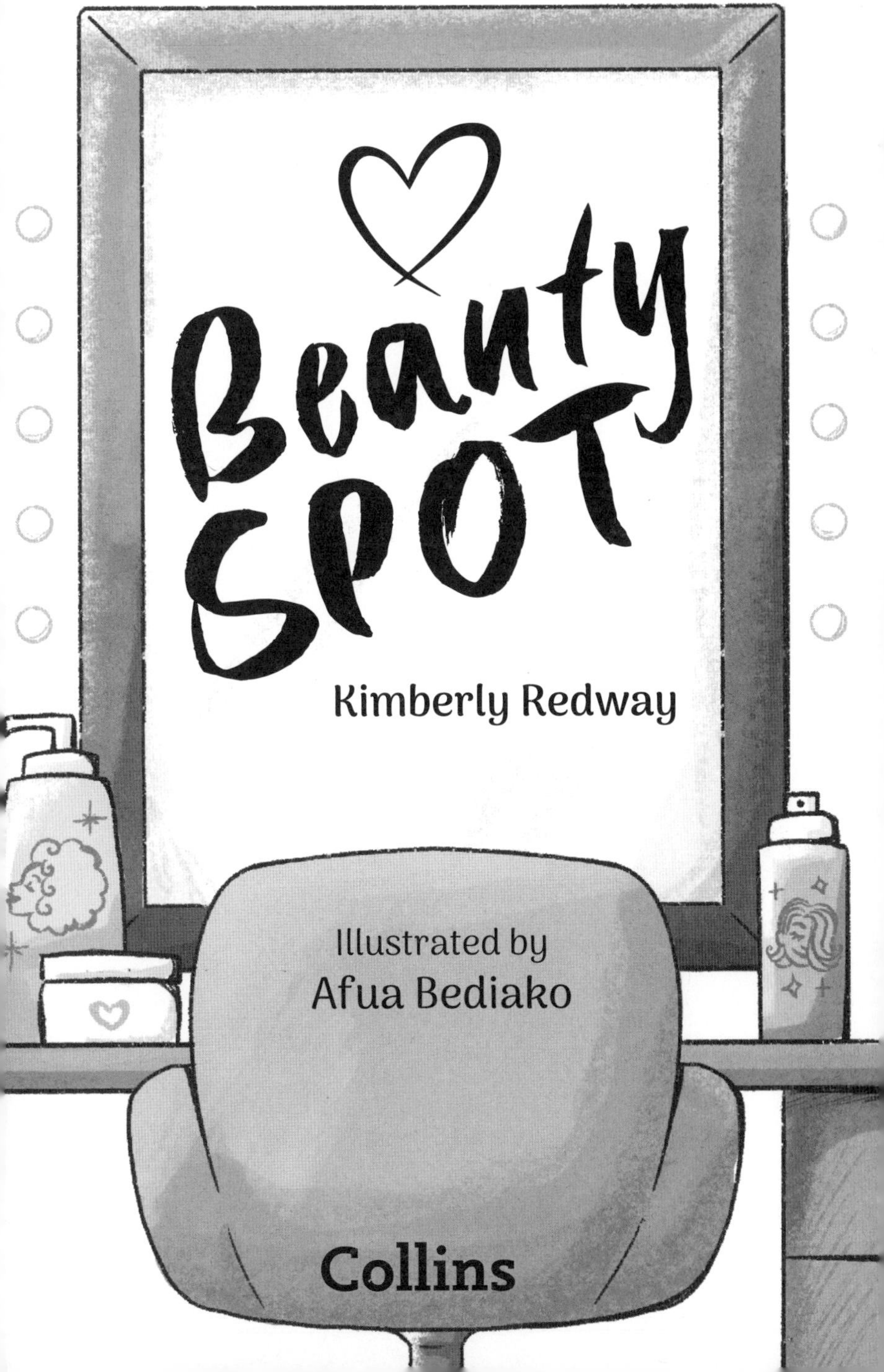

Beauty Spot
Kimberly Redway
Illustrated by
Afua Bediako
Collins

Chapter 1

Mum's a hair artist and she owns a hairdressing salon called Cuts & Locks. She knows how to twist locks and hold them up, so they almost defy gravity. She plays with the curly strands of an Afro and ties them back in canerows. She plaits long braids that swish down the backs of her customers. She dyes hair candy-floss pink and auburn; she slicks back hair with grease and steams natural hair. She says it's all beautiful.

Mum said when she was younger, Nanna Pearl would press her hair super straight. Now Mum's hair is dyed blonde and it falls in thick locks.

My name's Emerald, but everyone calls me Emmie. Mum said she named me and my older sister Amber after precious stones because we matter

to her. We live right next door to Cuts & Locks, in a row of large, terraced houses and flats. Mum painted our front door bright red and there's a gold knocker. We've got a small front garden with a rose bush that flowers in the summer.

Cuts & Locks is filled with large mirrors, shiny sinks and huge hairdryers. There are trays of hairdressing tools: combs, scissors and rollers. On the wall, there are shelves with lots of different bottles of shampoo and hairspray.

I was sitting in the corner of Cuts & Locks reading, as Mum steamed Leah's mum's hair. I was waiting for the whirlwind that was my Nanna Pearl. Suddenly, the bell above the shop door rang, and there she was. You couldn't miss her; she was wearing bright red trousers and a white shirt. Nanna Pearl's eyes seemed to be shining in the bright light of the hairdresser's, and they looked a little damp.

"Child, come and hug your nan," she said, with

a familiar bright smile on her face. I jumped up and put my arms around her. She smelt of something she called vanilla perfume. It was sweet and made me grin. She was finally here!

Nanna Pearl bustled around the shop, moving magazines and smiling at Mum and Auntie Gemma.

"How was France?" Mum asked.

"It was lovely," Nanna Pearl said. "I love Paris, but nothing's as brilliant as being with my favourite girls. Where's Amber?"

"She's at home," Mum said. She pressed her lips together until they almost disappeared. "She says she just wants to be by herself."

Amber had been away. No one talked about it, and I didn't know why. All I knew was that I'd missed her terribly and wanted to know what had happened. Whenever I asked Mum about it, she would press her lips together like she was doing now. I was determined to discover where she'd gone but even Amber wouldn't tell me.

"Well," Nanna Pearl said. "We'll have to see what we can do about that." She turned to me. "I'm coming to live with you for a little while, Emmie. How do you feel about that?"

"You mean it?" I asked, excitedly.

Nanna Pearl grinned. She rushed over to the small radio at the back of the shop. Suddenly, loud music came on. Auntie Gemma began swaying

and clicking her fingers. Mum danced about, moving from side to side.

Auntie Gemma's a family friend; she's known Mum for 15 years. When Mum set up Cuts & Locks five years ago, she couldn't wait to join. Uncle Paul also works here – he's another family friend. He danced as he put his coat on before he left for the day, giving us a cheery wave.

"What's this music?" I asked.

All three of them turned to look at me.

"It's reggae, Emmie," Nanna Pearl said, her mouth opening wide. "I can see I'm *definitely* needed here. Come and dance."

Mum shook her head. "This takes me back."

"Back to where?" I asked.

"I remember we used to come home after school," Mum said. "The music would be pounding, and we'd get ready for dinner. Nanna Pearl would be dancing while she cooked."

I copied Mum and danced from side to side.

“She’s got some moves,” Nanna Pearl said, looking at me. She twirled me around and we swayed to the music.

The bell over the shop door rang and Amber walked in. My older sister had her hair in braids which she always wore in a head wrap. She was dressed all in black – it was the only colour she wore these days. She used to wear lip gloss, and eyeshadow in so many different colours, but now she didn't bother.

"Nanna Pearl!" Amber shrieked. She rushed over and threw her arms around her. There were tears in my sister's eyes. "I can't believe you're here."

"Yes, I am," Nanna Pearl said. "And I won't be leaving for a while. I'm staying with you."

"That's great," Amber said.

Mum went over to Leah's mum and finished off her hair.

Nanna Pearl told us all about Paris. Of course, she'd seen the Eiffel Tower and gone to art galleries. She'd eaten at the best cafés and watched people walking past. I want to go there one day!

"That's Leah's mum," I whispered to Nanna Pearl, nodding to where Mum was working.

"Who's Leah?" Nanna Pearl asked.

"She's in my class," I said. "There's a group

called The Besties, because they're best friends, and she's part of it. There's Leah, Alexia and Jaspreet. They're so cool. I wish I was in The Besties."

"Why don't you ask them?" Nanna Pearl asked.

"I have. But I can't be in their group because I'm bigger than them," I said.

Nanna Pearl's eyes narrowed. "Who said that?"

"Leah," I said. "But it doesn't matter."

"I'm going to have a word with Leah's mum," Nanna Pearl said. We both looked over to where Leah's mum had been sitting, but she'd already left without us noticing.

"That's not very nice," Amber said. She was sitting opposite me and hugging her legs. "You should be able to join in."

I shrugged as Mum walked over to us.

"Leah's been telling Emmie she's too big," Nanna Pearl said.

"What?" Mum asked.

I wanted to go back to reading my book about cities. I wanted to crawl into the pages and hang around with the characters. I didn't want to think about being different. I didn't want to think about how the other girls were thinner than me.

"I'll talk to Leah's mum," Mum said. She sounded like Nanna Pearl. "It's a shame she's just left."

"You can't," I said. "It doesn't matter."

"Of course it does, because it's made you sad," Mum told me. "I won't have you upset, love."

"I'm going to go home," Amber said. She had a pinched look on her face, and she looked as though she might cry.

"What's wrong?" Mum asked her.

But Amber didn't answer. She got up and walked out of the shop.

"She's always like that now," Mum said, softly.

"I never know the right thing to say."

"It was never going to be easy," Nanna Pearl replied, giving Mum a hug. "It's all about her getting better now. Don't forget I'm here. Let's get on home, there's something I need to show Emmie."

Chapter 2

When we got home, Nanna Pearl asked me to help her unpack her things. She sat me down on the bed and looked a bit serious. I wondered what Nanna Pearl wanted to show me. *Is it in her bag*? I wondered. Maybe it's a long necklace made of pearls, or a purple hat with a feather in it. Nanna Pearl always wore brilliant clothes that stood out.

"Emmie, does an emerald gemstone look exactly like an amber gemstone?" Nanna Pearl asked me.

"No," I said.

"Does that make one better than the other?" Nanna Pearl then asked.

I shook my head.

“Correct! They’re both different and yet both are precious. I want to show you something.” She held up a mirror and I looked into it. My hair was in two Afro puffs pulled away from my face. My skin was dark brown, and my eyes were wide and seemed to sparkle in the light.

“Can you see that dot on your face?” Nanna Pearl asked.

I nodded.

"It's called a beauty spot," Nanna Pearl said. "Whatever you feel about yourself in this moment and the future, I want you to understand that no two people are the same. But I don't want you to see that as a bad thing. It's a wonderful thing. Your mind, your sense of humour and your looks are different from everyone else's. That's what makes us human."

"But I'm bigger than everyone else," I said, and sighed.

Nanna Pearl thought for a moment. "Would you be happy, do you think, if you ate the same thing every day?"

"No, I'd get bored," I said.

"It's the same with people," Nanna Pearl said, and she gave a shout of laughter. "I bet Leah's different from her friends, isn't she? She doesn't look or sound the same as the other girls – yes? Yet they managed to find common ground. That's why they connect."

"They all like dancing," I said. "They do dances in the playground at school."

Nanna Pearl had a look on her face then. I recognised it as the one she always had when she got an idea.

"Do you like dancing?" she asked.

I shrugged, but deep down I wanted to shout "Yes!"

"I seem to remember you dancing along to reggae just a moment ago," Nanna Pearl said. She pressed her sleek grey bob down with her hands. Then she began to dance a little. "Dancing is fun, isn't it?"

I nodded.

"I think you need time to get to know yourself. I propose that we take you to a dance class. That will be step number one."

"What's step number two?" I asked. But she tapped her nose which meant, I'll tell you when I'm ready.

That evening, we ate roast chicken for dinner and, for a bit of flair, rice and peas. We sat at the huge table which took up a lot of the space in the kitchen.

Dad had cooked today, and he served up the food onto plates. Eating at home used to be full of noise; we would talk about the day and sometimes Amber would start singing a song. But lately there was just silence. Now I think about it, it's been like this since just before Amber went away. I looked over at her; Amber's face looked tight as she slowly ate.

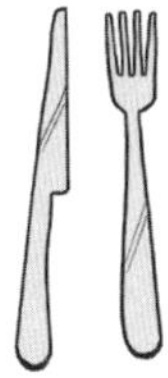

Mum and Dad kept exchanging glances and watching my sister.

Nanna Pearl ate for a while and then sighed loudly. "This won't do," she said. She rushed out of the room and returned with a small radio. It was red and shiny with silver knobs on it. "Let's liven things up." Nanna Pearl turned the knobs, and reggae played again. She clicked her fingers and began singing along.

Amber looked up slowly from her plate. Then she dropped her

knife and fork onto her plate with a clatter. As we all turned to look at her, she pushed her plate away and walked out of the room.

Mum closed her eyes for a moment and then got up and followed after her. I looked at Dad; he put his fork down and took my hand. He gave me a small smile, but it didn't reach his eyes.

"Is Amber, OK?" I asked.

"It's going to take time ... for her to get better," Dad said.

"*What's* going to take time?" I asked. I stared at him as though I could see the answer on his face. Would he tell me what was happening now?

"Amber will tell you in her own time," he said. "She said she wants to talk to you about it, but you'll have to wait until she's ready."

We continued to eat, and soon the thumping music from the radio seemed to move through me. I started clicking my fingers and nodding my head. Dad began singing along.

I'd always been close to Amber. In the winter, we always made a huge snowman together and used Dad's hat and scarf to keep it warm. In the summer, Mum and Dad would take us to the beach, and we built sandcastles with buckets and spades. I missed sitting with her on the sofa in the living room with steaming hot chocolates. We'd watch films, and Dad would do funny voices, pretending to be the actors.

Now Amber would sit by herself, wrapped in her baggy cardigan. She would scroll on her phone

sometimes, and if I spoke to her, she'd huff. "Sorry, Emmie," she'd say. "I'm busy."

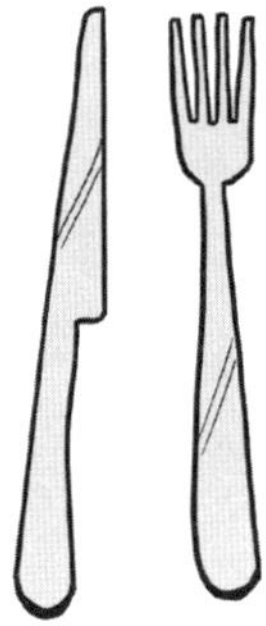

It made me sad to think about this. Amber came back to the table and sat down next to me. She ate slowly.

"I'm going to take Emmie to a dance class," Nanna Pearl announced.

"What kind?" Dad asked.

"Ballet would be amazing, don't you think?" Nanna Pearl said. "I believe Emmie will be brilliant at it."

"It's a great idea," Mum smiled.

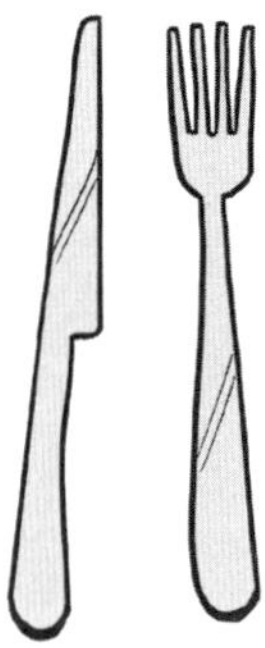

"Yeah," Amber said. She looked over at me and we smiled at each other.

"I still need to talk to Leah's mum," Mum said. She looked stern and her eyebrows lowered. "We'll see what Leah has to say for herself. I'm also going to tell Ms Bell."

Ms Bell was my class teacher. I looked down at my dinner. What would Leah say?

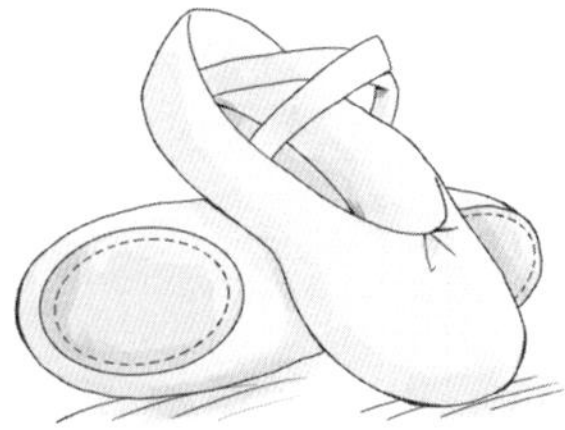

Chapter 3

"We're The Besties," Leah, Jaspreet and Alexia shouted. Whenever we heard those words, lots of the girls in my class would follow them to the back of the playground. A few of the boys would join too, and everyone would whoop and shout. There were a couple of steps in the upper school playground where the three girls stood; when everyone was watching, they'd begin singing.

Leah was the superstar of the group. They sang the coolest songs; Leah sang the loudest and danced in front while Jaspreet and Alexia were backup singers. When they finished, they posed, and everyone clapped enthusiastically.

Leah was Black and had ringlets that bounced around her face. Jaspreet was Indian and

she had her hair in two plaits with a chopped fringe. Alexia was White and had her blonde hair in a ponytail. Nanna Pearl was right; they were different in their own way. Yet, they all liked singing and dancing. I watched them, and my heart pounded. Mum had spoken to Leah's mum last night.

"Leah's mum will speak to her," Mum had said. I'd shrunk down on the sofa when she told me.

"OK, that's enough now," Ms Bell said. "Emmie, Leah, Jaspreet and Alexia. Come with me, please."

I followed after our teacher. Jaspreet kept looking at me, but I looked straight ahead. What was Ms Bell going to say? We went into the classroom.

"Sit down," Ms Bell said. "It's come to my attention that some of you girls have been making personal remarks about others. Leah, did you say that Emmie is too big?"

I couldn't look at anyone. I looked down at my hands. I opened and closed them.

"Yes," Leah admitted. "Why?"

"It's not a very nice thing to say," Ms Bell said. "Do you remember the assembly about respecting each other? We should be celebrating each other's differences. It isn't kind to exclude people

from playing with you. Is it?"

"No," Leah said, softly.

"Emmie was very upset," Ms Bell said. "I want you three to apologise to her."

"Sorry," they chorused.

"Right, you can go back outside now," Ms Bell said.

Leah and Alexia rushed off outside, but

Jaspreet walked slowly with me.

"Sorry about not letting you in the group, Emmie," Jaspreet said.

I looked at her. "It's OK," I said. "Your dance routine was really cool."

"Thanks," she said. "How's Amber? My mum said she wasn't well but she's getting better now."

"I don't know what was wrong," I said.

Jaspreet looked thoughtful. "Oh. Maybe you should ask her."

We walked in silence for a moment.

"I know," Jaspreet said. "Why don't you write her a letter?"

"Just like in the lesson we had," I said.

Ms Bell had taught a lesson where we wrote letters to famous people from history. I'd chosen to write to Queen Elizabeth I.

"That's a good idea," I said.

“Cool,” Jaspreet replied, as we reached the door to the playground. I saw Leah and Alexia standing way off watching us. “Anyway, see you later.”

She grinned and ran off to join her friends. I stood watching the three of them do a special handshake and then they sat down together on the benches. In that instant, I made myself a promise that I would be part of The Besties. I wanted so badly to have a secret handshake and to be popular. I knew this would happen if I joined The Besties. I wanted to dance with them; their routines looked so great.

At the end of school, Nanna Pearl met me at the school gates. She was holding a drawstring bag. "Your mum is with Amber," she said. "So, I'm here to take you to your first dance class."

I didn't know that Nanna Pearl would get me into a dance class this quickly, but I knew she had a way of getting things done. If I learnt how to dance, The Besties might let me join them. I felt like I was fizzing with excitement; I could barely stand still at the thought of something new.

"The dance teacher will lend you some shoes for this lesson," Nanna Pearl said.

We walked together to a huge building. Inside, there was a room with large mirrors and railings around it. Nanna Pearl said they were called barres. A woman walked over; she looked stern at first, but then her face broke into a smile at the sight of us. She was dressed in white tracksuit bottoms and what Nanna Pearl called a black "leotard".

"I'm Sabrina," she said. "Welcome to your first dance class. You must be Emmie."

Nanna Pearl opened the drawstring bag and handed me a leotard that used to belong to Amber. Then she sat at the back of the hall, and I went to the changing room. When I returned to the hall, Sabrina offered me some soft ballet shoes.

"Come and meet everyone else," she said.

I walked over to the other girls who were all around my age. They smiled, and then I saw someone I recognised. Jaspreet. There was no sign of Leah or Alexia. I rushed over.

"Hey, Emmie," Jaspreet said, grinning. "You're going to have so much fun here."

Sabrina introduced me to the class and then we started with some stretches; I had some simpler ones to do as I was new. It reminded me of PE. The others were preparing for a dance showcase in a few days, so Sabrina put on the music and took them through the routine.

"I'm going to give you a part," Sabrina told me. "You'll need to learn a few steps and that will get you settled in, OK? I'll teach you a bit more after class so you can catch up."

I felt so good about what I learnt, and it felt good to move around in such a large space.

It was also brilliant to be with the other dancers. Everyone was included.

"I want you to enjoy the feeling of movement," Sabrina said, at the end of the class. "I want you to feel strong and powerful with every step you take. Your dance will tell the story to the audience and pull them into a moment that you create."

"You did so well," Jaspreet said to me, at the end.

"Thanks," I said. "When I get home, I'm going to write a letter to Amber."

Nanna Pearl took me home, but when we got near, we could hear shouting coming from inside the house. We opened the door quietly; Mum and Amber were in the living room.

"You want me to be perfect and I'm not," Amber was saying.

"Amber, it's not about perfection," Mum answered. "I want you to be OK. Talk to me."

"I'm so tired all the time. I know I'm getting better, Mum. I'm glad to get help, I just wish it was faster," Amber was saying. Her cardigan hung off her shoulders and her eyes were filled with tears. When she noticed me and Nanna Pearl, she ran upstairs.

Mum looked distraught. "I'm just not sure what to do," she said. Nanna Pearl folded her in a tight hug.

Chapter 4

I did know what to do. I found a piece of lined paper and began writing my letter.

Dear Amber,

I'm writing this to you because you're sad and I want you to be happy again. Dad said it will take time, but I want to know what's wrong. Please tell me.

I remember when we went on the caravan holiday. You won the singing competition. Now you barely sing any more. I want you to be OK. Please write back.

Love, Emmie

I folded up the letter and wrote, "To Amber" on it. I put it outside her bedroom door and knocked. Before she came out, I ran to my own bedroom and closed the door.

Before bedtime, there was a knock on my door. I opened it and there was a letter on the carpet. "To Emmie" was written on the folded-up paper.

Dear Emmie,

Thanks for your letter. It was good to get post!

I'm sorry I've not talked to you very much. I want to tell you what's been happening to me and why I went away. I want to get better for you and for myself.

The first thing is, I don't always like how I look. That's why I was upset when I heard what Leah said to you. I don't want anyone to make you feel bad about how you look. If you want, you can write me another letter.

Love, Amber

The next morning, I quickly wrote another letter to Amber. I put it by her bedroom door.

Dear Amber,

I didn't know you felt different! I feel different all the time. I'm bigger than the other girls in my class. Nanna Pearl said difference is good and we can't all be the same. I don't like getting changed in PE. I rush to do it. Sometimes, I wish I looked like Leah.

Love, Emmie

I couldn't believe I'd finally told someone how I felt. I was glad I could write down my feelings in a letter and give it to Amber. What would she think?

All through my school lessons, I could barely concentrate. Amber and I look different but we both don't like how we look. Maybe we could help each other? What would Amber think about what I'd written to her. Would she think I was silly?

When I got home, I saw Amber. She was dressed in her navy school uniform for secondary school, so she must have gone in today. She hugged me close and handed me a letter.

"Read what I wrote then come and speak to me after dinner," she said. I could hear her singing softly, as I walked back to my room with the letter.

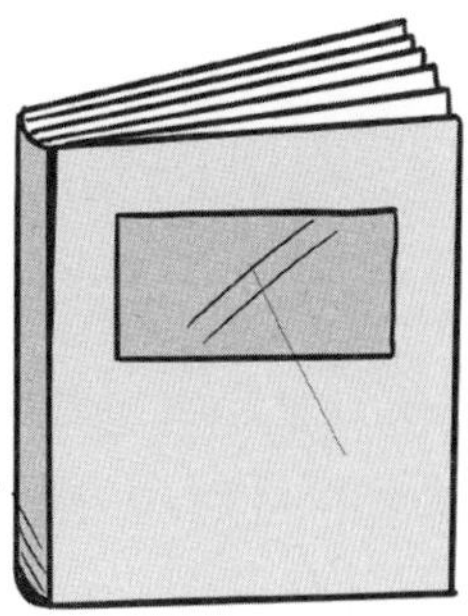

Dear Emmie,

Wow, I totally understand how you feel. At school, Miss Lyn said that bodies come in all shapes and sizes. Sometimes people feel like they want to change their bodies or look like someone else. That's what I want to say to you, Emmie. I love how you look, and that might not mean much. I want you to see what I see. I want you to look in the mirror and feel positive about yourself.

I keep thinking about this. When I was away for those three months, I had lots of time to think. I thought about my body. I thought about how unusual and different I feel. I never thought about how you feel about yourself. So, after dinner, I'm going to tell you what happened to me. Thanks for being the most awesome sister in the world, and let's keep writing letters. It's so fun.

Love, Amber

Everyone was sitting at the kitchen table when I walked in. Amber was now dressed in her baggy cardigan and jeans. Her face brightened as I entered the room.

"Can I choose the music?" she asked Nanna Pearl, who'd brought her red radio to the kitchen again.

Nanna Pearl nodded.

Amber changed the channel and a song we knew well came on. She began singing in her deep beautiful voice. She has always been an amazing singer; her voice sounded just like the pop star's, and at the end we all clapped. Amber hid her face

in mock embarrassment.

"Oh Amber, that was sensational," Mum said.

Today, we had lasagne and salad. We ate and chatted again like we used to.

"Did Ms Bell speak to you?" Mum asked.

"That was yesterday. Leah, Jaspreet and Alexia apologised," I said.

"I'm going to tell Emmie about why I went away," Amber said to Mum.

"That's great," Mum replied. She took Amber's hand. "When you're done, I want us to all have a chat about it."

Amber nodded.

In that moment, I thought about the times when Mum or Dad would go to see Amber. I'd stay at home and wonder; I wanted to know what had happened to her. I remember how we always used to watch TV together as a family. Now, Mum and Dad didn't always have the time. Everything was different. It was time to find out what was going on.

Chapter 5

I went into Amber's room after dinner and sat on her bed. I hadn't been in her room for ages; soft music was coming from her laptop, and the most glorious clothes spilt out of the wardrobe. She had pictures of singers on a collage she'd made in Art class on the wall.

"Do you know what an eating disorder is?" Amber asked me.

I shook my head.

"Well, that's what I have," Amber said. "I wanted to change how I looked, and I believed that if I didn't eat, I'd get what I wanted. Mum and Dad finally worked out what was happening and tried to help me. I was trying to hide it, but they knew."

Her eyes filled with tears which she wiped away.

"I didn't want to go away at all," she said. "I didn't want to leave my friends, but I needed to get better. I shouldn't have shouted at Mum the other day."

We sat in silence together for a moment. The music changed to another track.

"Why did you want to change how you looked?" I asked her.

"Because of how I see myself," she said. "And that's why I wanted to talk to you, face to face. Seeing how you feel about yourself has made me realise the truth. Beauty isn't just one thing. Nanna Pearl talked to me too. That's kind of why she's here. She wants us to explore what we feel about how we look and to make sure we see ourselves in a positive way. She wants us to be confident about who we are even when our brain is telling us something else."

"So, you don't think it's silly that I want to look like Leah?" I asked.

"Of course not," she said. "It's how you feel, but I think Nanna Pearl wants us to consider *why* we feel the way we do."

"And do you feel better now?" I asked her.

"I have up and down times," she said. "That's why I'm grateful for all your support. And for your letters. I'm feeling a lot better, and I talk about it with a counsellor."

We hugged – I was hoping I could give Amber some positive vibes with my hug, and I think she was doing the same for me.

"Come on, I think Mum wants to speak to us about it," she said.

We went downstairs to the living room, and I groaned. Mum had out the comb, hair grease and a determined expression on her face. Amber chuckled and sat down next to Mum.

Changing my hairstyle wasn't always pleasant. I sat on the floor as Mum undid my hairbands and began combing my hair. She put it into sections by parting it. Once this was done, she began the task of canerowing it. She liked to do zig-zag patterns all through my hair, and then she would tie the ends and comb out the puffs.

"There's a lot of things we've not really spoken about as a family," Mum said, as she began doing my hair. "I'm glad you two have had a chat about what's going on."

"I told Amber that sometimes I wish I looked like Leah," I said.

"That's why I'm glad Nanna Pearl is taking you to ballet," Mum said. "It's a chance to explore a whole new skill. It's easy to imagine there's a way to measure beauty, but you can't compare a stork to a pelican. They're different. It can be easy to compare ourselves to other people but it's important we find those things that we love about ourselves too."

"Mum, did you always like how you looked?" Amber asked.

"Not always. Growing up, there were things I didn't like about my body," Mum said.

"Really?" I asked Mum. I turned to face her, shocked. I never knew she felt like this. Mum was confident. She danced around the house. She did exercises in the middle of the living room. She stretched up to the ceiling and touched her toes. She wore bold colours and walked down the street like it was a runway.

"As I grew up, I had to adjust," she said. "There are lots of changes you go through as a teen – everyone goes through that. But I was also bigger than the other girls in my class."

My mouth dropped open. Why had she never said anything?

"I wish I'd talked through all of this with you two," Mum said. "But we'll have these talks now. We'll speak through it all."

I leant back against Mum's legs, and she continued to comb my hair.

"I'm glad you talked to Emmie," Mum told Amber. "I want us to be open about our feelings."

Nanna Pearl walked in and caught the end of the conversation. "I have an exercise for us to do after school tomorrow," she said. "It's time for step number two."

Chapter 6

I was sitting in the school playground reading a book, when Leah, Jaspreet and Alexia walked over. Jaspreet was biting her lip.

Leah stood in front of me, with one hand on her hip. "I've been thinking about this for a couple of days, Emmie. I can't believe you told your mum about what I said." She pouted. "Why do you even care?"

I just stared at her. I wanted to say all the things Nanna Pearl and Mum had said. That being different wasn't a terrible thing. But I couldn't seem to find the right words.

"Well?" Leah snapped.

"Well, what you said wasn't very nice, Leah," Jaspreet said. "Besides, I don't see why Emmie can't be part of The Besties. She's really fun."

"Why are you standing up for her?" Alexia asked. "We're your friends, not her."

"Because you're not being kind," Jaspreet said. "And you're not being fair."

"Why don't you like me, Leah?" I asked, softly.

"Because you got me into trouble," Leah said. "Come on, Alexia. Jaspreet, you're not in the group any more."

"What? But why?" Jaspreet asked.

"Because if you think I'm not kind or fair, then maybe we can't be friends any more," Leah said. She stomped off.

Alexia shrugged, and then followed after Leah.

Jaspreet sighed and sat next to me. Then she began to cry; I put my arm around her.

"Leah's my best friend," Jaspreet said. "But what she said wasn't nice and she doesn't seem sorry."

I can remember the first day I saw The Besties

dance in the playground. I wanted to be part of it from that moment. I couldn't imagine the group breaking up.

"I'm sorry, Jaspreet," I said. "Thanks for sticking up for me."

"It's OK," she said, wiping her eyes.

We sat in silence for a moment. I looked at a group of kids across the playground. Jaspreet looked at the book that was next to me on the bench.

"You're reading?" she asked, as though she was confused.

"Yeah," I said. "I like to read at breaktime."

"Why?" she asked. "Why aren't you hanging around with your friends?"

Suddenly, her eyebrows lowered as she looked at me. Her eyes were still glittering with tears, and she chewed her lip thoughtfully.

"You do have friends, right?" she asked.

"I used to be friends with Lily, but she went to another school," I said.

"Oh," Jaspreet said. "Hey, how about we be friends? We could have so much fun. And we're doing ballet together."

Jaspreet was right, I thought, as she grinned at me. We had something in common – we went to the same dance class.

"I'd like to be your friend," I said. "Also, thanks for your advice about writing a letter to Amber."

"You're welcome," Jaspreet said, smiling.

Lily had been my best friend. We'd gone to each other's houses and our families had gone on trips together. Sometimes, we'd sit together reading books. Thinking of Lily gave me an idea.

"I know! Let's make up a dance routine of our own before the bell goes," I said.

"That would be so awesome," Jaspreet said.

Jaspreet showed me some ballet moves I hadn't learnt yet, and I showed her how Nanna Pearl danced to reggae music.

After break, Leah and Alexia sat together in class. They whispered and kept looking at Jaspreet; I kept watching Jaspreet's face. She was no longer crying, but she looked unbearably sad. She'd defended me, and it was as though she was being punished for being nice to me.

Ms Bell had invited all the parents in to see our artwork. After school, everyone walked around the classroom and looked at the displays. Jaspreet had done a huge painting of a ballet dancer with a pink tutu. I'd done a painting of me and Amber sitting together. Mum said it was beautiful.

As we filed out into the playground, I heard Jaspreet's mum say to her, "Aren't you friends with Leah?"

I saw some of the other mums and dads look around at her.

"We had a ... falling-out," Jaspreet said. She looked at the ground.

"Come on, let's sort this out," Jaspreet's mum said. I saw her walk over to Leah and her mum.

"What's going on with Leah and Jaspreet?" Mum asked me.

"Alexia and Leah stopped talking to Jaspreet because she stood up for me after they were mean to me," I said.

"Right, let's get to the bottom of this," Mum said. We walked over to where Leah, Jaspreet and Alexia were standing with their mums.

"What's happened?" we heard Leah's mum ask.

"Jaspreet and Leah had a falling-out," Jaspreet's mum said, shaking her head.

"It's because Leah said Emmie was too big to join our dance group," Jaspreet said.

Everyone turned to look at me.

Leah's mum sighed. "I thought we'd sorted this out."

"Oh dear," Alexia's mum said. She looked stern.

"Why don't you all come to my salon. We can have a hot drink and a chat," Mum said.

The mums all nodded in agreement. We walked to Cuts & Locks and entered through the back door. I could hear the soft chatter of Mum's customers and smell hairspray. Mum arranged some chairs, and we all sat together. Mum had called Nanna Pearl to let her know we were on our way, and she, Auntie Gemma and Amber joined us.

"Leah and Jaspreet have fallen out," I whispered to Amber. "Mum's invited everyone here to have a chat."

"I bet Nanna Pearl will sort it out," Amber said back. "She always has good ideas."

I could see Mum saying something to Nanna Pearl.

"Right," Nanna Pearl said. "I'm glad we're all here. I have an idea for an exercise. I'm just going

to see if your mums want to have a go."

The mums got up from their seats and crowded round Nanna Pearl. They spoke excitedly about something, but I couldn't quite hear. Then they came back to their seats. Mum went to the small kitchen area and returned with teas and coffees for the mums. There was juice for us.

"Right, this is an exercise about differences," Nanna Pearl said. "I want you girls to say something nice about someone sitting near you. We'll go around the room. We'll start with Emmie."

"I like the freckles on Alexia's arm," I said, softly. I looked around; everyone was looking at me encouragingly, so I lifted my voice a little. "They really stand out."

"Thanks, Emmie," Alexia said. "Am I next?"

Nanna Pearl nodded. "Yes, it's your turn," she said.

"I really like Leah's hair," Alexia said. "When it isn't braided, it's really curly."

Leah's mum smiled. "That's a lovely thing to say about Leah, Alexia. I remember my mum trying to put a hat over my hair," she said and then laughed. "I could barely get it on. It's fun to have different hairstyles for my Afro hair. I also love when Emmie's mum braids it."

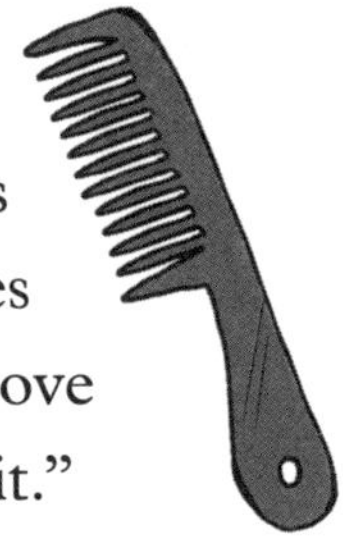

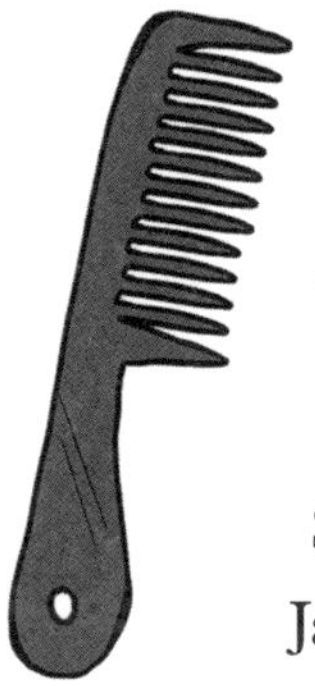

"I think I'm next," Leah said. She thought for a moment. "I like Jaspreet's smile."

"Thanks, Leah," Jaspreet said. She smiled wide and I saw what Leah meant.

It was Jaspreet's turn. "I love Emmie's beauty spot," Jaspreet said. "It's so amazing. I wish I had one."

"You mean it?" I asked Jaspreet.

Jaspreet nodded.

"I have all sorts of women come into my hairdresser's,"

Mum said. "Some have curly auburn hair, some have long thick Afro hair, some even come in with mohawks. I really love seeing it all. There's beauty in this difference. Imagine if I had to do the same style every day, I'm sure I'd get bored. I guess what I'm trying to say is, I love what you've all said about each other."

Nanna Pearl put her hand on Mum's shoulder. "We all change as we get older. I want you girls to feel confident in who you are."

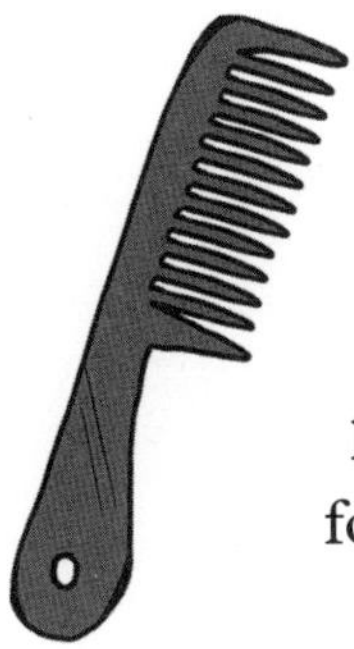

"I know it's up to you who your friends are," Amber said, looking at Jaspreet and Alexia. "But I hope there might be a place in your friendship group for Emmie."

"I'm sorry I was unkind to you, Jaspreet," Leah said. "And I'm also sorry to you, Emmie. Do you want to be part of The Besties?"

It was all I'd ever wanted. "Of course!" I said.

Chapter 7

The four of us decided to make up a new dance so we went to Leah's house after the hairdresser's. Leah's family lived in a ground floor flat near us, but I'd not been there before. There was a huge wooden coffee table that Leah's mum had pushed out of the way so we could dance.

"I saw you two dancing in the playground," Leah said to me and Jaspreet. "You should show us some moves."

"Sure," Jaspreet said.

"Ready," Leah said, and then we all shouted. "We are … The Besties."

Leah had music playing in the background and we came up with ideas for steps. We all decided that on Friday we'd perform a new routine. We had to get it just right.

"How about we jump forward and then run back?" Jaspreet asked.

"Then turn and pose," Alexia said.

"What about this?" I waggled my finger and sashayed about.

"You're so funny, Emmie," Alexia said, giggling.

We built the dance routine, move by move. We worked until we were all laughing. When I went home, I wrote a letter to Amber.

Dear Amber,

I can't believe I'm part of The Besties! Thanks so much for asking them if I could join.

I know Mum said it will take time for you to get better. I've really enjoyed writing these letters to you.

Love, Emmie

Amber was sitting in the living room with her cardigan wrapped around her. She always hid in her cardigan, but it seemed she was doing this less and less now. She looked tired but happy as I handed her the letter and went to see Nanna Pearl.

"Ah, Emmie," Nanna Pearl said, as I walked into the kitchen. "I'm glad you're now friends with those girls. Wasn't it good to hear what you all liked about each other? Oh, and Emmie, don't forget I'll be taking you to ballet tomorrow."

She moved over to the radio and turned it up. The familiar sound of reggae filled the kitchen. She put out a hand for me to take. "Come and dance with me," she said.

I did some of the moves I'd practised with The Besties; Amber came into the kitchen and joined us. We bounced about on our feet and had a mini dance party. After a while, Nanna Pearl sat down on a chair and fanned herself with her hand.

"Nanna Pearl gave us an exercise to do," Amber said to me. "Come on – this is step number two."

We sat in the living room with pads of paper on our laps. I waited for Amber to tell me what we were doing.

"So, Nanna Pearl said to write what we're grateful for," Amber said. She dangled a leg off the sofa. "So, let's do that."

Here's what I wrote.

I'm grateful for ...

Mum and Dad.

I'm glad Nanna Pearl has come to visit.

I'm so pleased Amber's feeling better.

I'm also grateful for my beauty spot ...

"How's it going?" Nanna Pearl asked, coming into the room.

"It's hard to think," I said. "I am grateful, but it's hard to write it down."

"Don't worry, this is a new exercise," Nanna Pearl said. "You don't have to get it done straight away. You can keep the paper, and every time something happens, you can add it to the list. How about you, Amber?"

Amber looked up. There were tears in her eyes; they fell down her face onto the paper. "I am grateful," she said. "I just ... I wish I was never ill. I missed you all so much when I was away. Sometimes, I wonder why it happened to me."

Nanna Pearl sat next to Amber and hugged her.

"Right now, what matters is that you're here with us," Nanna Pearl said. "What things are you grateful for. Do you mind sharing?"

"Well, my family," Amber said. "My friends at school have been great. I'm glad for the people who took care of me and helped me. I'm just ... I'm still struggling with how I feel about my body. I want to put it on my list. I want to be thankful. But it's like Emmie said. Sometimes, I compare myself to my friends. Nanna Pearl, will I ever stop thinking like this?"

"Comparing yourself with others is natural," Nanna Pearl said. "But it's going to take time for – "

"Me to get better, I know," Amber said, finishing Nanna Pearl's sentence.

"Do you think I'm confident?" Nanna Pearl asked me and Amber.

We nodded.

"Well, I wasn't always," Nanna Pearl said. "When I was younger, there was a girl in my class called Ruth. She was tall and she was good at a lot of subjects. I wanted to be just like her."

"How did you stop comparing yourself to her?" Amber asked.

"It took a while," Nanna Pearl said. "But it came by realising that I had my own unique way of doing things and presenting myself. So that's what I'm trying to teach you two. I know it'll take time, Amber, because it took me time to appreciate that I have my own skills, my own talents, my own way of moving through the world."

"What's your talent?" Amber asked.

"Well, I'm a great dancer, if you can't tell," Nanna Pearl said, laughing. "I'm also a good singer. But I dance better than I sing; I'm not as talented as you."

"Let's sing a song," I said.

Amber looked over at me. She'd wiped her eyes and was looking a little happier. "I'll get my laptop," she said.

"What about the radio?" Nanna Pearl asked.

"All of my best songs are on the laptop," Amber said.

"How about an oldie so I'll know the words?" Nanna Pearl asked.

"OK," Amber said. She pulled up a playlist on her laptop. A song came on. It was one that Mum liked, so we all knew the words.

"This really is an old one," I said.

Nanna Pearl smiled. "Come on, girls," she said.

We began singing, carefully trying to harmonise. Amber kept pretending to be a conductor and then she took charge. She began

telling us which parts to sing and how. We kept replaying the song until we were giggling. It reminded me of being part of The Besties.

When Amber was sure it was fine, she finally sat down.

"So, we have a singer and a dancer in the family?" Nanna Pearl said.

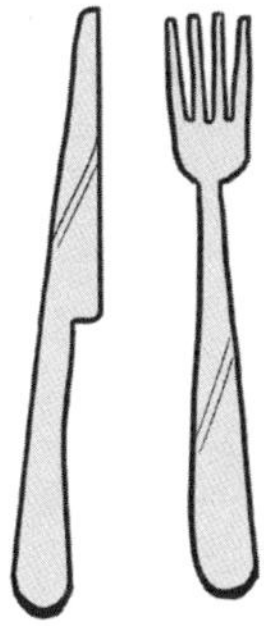

Mum poked her head round the door. "As long as you're getting your schoolwork done as well."

"Oh, Mum," Amber said, lying down on the sofa.

"We've got an appointment coming up, Amber," Mum said. "Don't forget."

"How can I?" Amber asked. "You never let me." Amber got up and walked out of the room. It was like the singing never happened, and I felt as though I was sinking. It had been so good and suddenly it was gone.

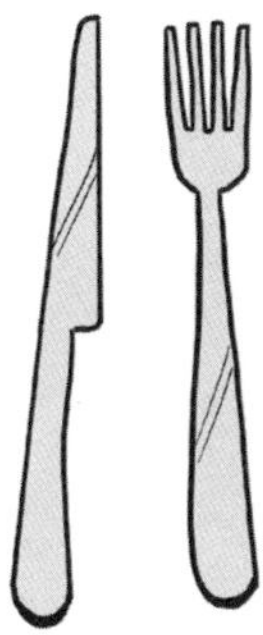

"I'll go after her," Nanna Pearl said.

I closed my eyes for a moment and wished it could be different.

After a while, Nanna Pearl returned with a letter from Amber for me.

Chapter 8

Dear Emmie,

It's hard to tell you exactly how I feel. I feel up and down sometimes, but I know one thing I'm grateful for. I'm grateful for a sister like you. I'm glad you have new friends; I have good friends, as well, and they're always looking out for me. I'm also grateful to be able to sing. I love singing, especially with you. I guess I haven't felt like doing it a lot lately. I'm sorry if I spoilt things just now.

Love, Amber

I didn't see Amber for the rest of the evening. Mum and Dad kept exchanging worried looks, and it reminded me of when Amber first came back after she'd been away. Nanna Pearl didn't put on the radio. She sat on the sofa with her eyes closed, but I knew she wasn't asleep. It wasn't like Nanna Pearl to be so quiet. Every so often, she would go upstairs to check on my sister. I kept rereading the words Amber had written.

I thought about the chance to write what we were grateful for. I added "The Besties" to my list. I had new friends now. I really hoped Amber was OK.

At ballet the next day, Sabrina got us to stretch and then we went through some dance steps: we did pliés; we had to bend our knees and straighten them out. It felt good to stretch and move my body into different positions. Everything was new and different. It was hard sometimes as I'd never done it before, but Sabrina always watched out for me.

"You can rest a bit, Emmie," she'd say.

Jaspreet was amazing at the moves as she'd been doing ballet for a while.

"You're doing amazingly well, Emmie," Sabrina said to me. "I want you to sit with me while the other girls perform the act. I'll show you your moves in a moment."

Sabrina started the music as we all stood together, ready to perform. Jaspreet was one of the lead dancers, and as she started to move, the stretching exercises made sense. The moves were elegant and beautiful. Jaspreet stretched and held her leg in the air. The dancers twirled and I could feel my body shifting with the music. I couldn't wait to be part of it.

Afterwards, Sabrina showed me my part. She counted out the beat and the other girls clapped as I began to learn what to do.

"That was fantastic, Emmie," Sabrina said.

Nanna Pearl came in a little early and put her hands over her eyes. "I want to be surprised when I see the final performance," she said.

"Emmie's doing really well," Sabrina said. "Her stretches are great, and she's got a part in the dance showcase."

She clapped her hands, and everyone stood up. “Right, let’s do the routine one more time today. I want everyone to stand tall, stretch as best you can, and I want you to give it your best effort. Emmie, I want you to join in, too. Remember what I showed you.”

The music began. My heart pounded a little

as I remembered what Sabrina had taught me. Suddenly, Jaspreet started moving and the others joined in. I began my steps and moved to the count that Sabrina called out, so we'd be on the beat. It happened in an instant: suddenly, I was Emerald, the amazing ballet dancer. I pointed my toes, I moved my arms and listened to the music. It felt wonderful.

I was enjoying myself so much I felt a little disappointed when the routine came to an end. I looked up and saw Amber standing next to Nanna Pearl.

It was as though I was coming out of a dream. Amber rushed over to me and hugged me. "That was awesome," she said.

"You're a natural," Nanna Pearl nodded. She was watching me, after all. "I knew you'd be fabulous."

We all got ready to go home and Sabrina came over to me, Amber and Nanna Pearl.

"Emmie's done a fantastic job," Sabrina said. "We have a few more lessons before the showcase but I'm confident Emmie will do well."

I felt like I was glowing. Nanna Pearl hugged me, and we left to go home.

"Make way for the champion ballet dancer," Nanna Pearl announced, as we walked into the house. "Emmie's going to win loads of awards someday. She'll be in lots of dance performances."

Mum chuckled. Dad looked at me with a proud smile.

"Are you enjoying it, Emmie?" Mum asked me.

"It was amazing," I said.

"You should see her," Nanna Pearl said.

Nanna Pearl put a concentrated look on her face and began to dance like a ballet dancer.

Amber copied her and I laughed.

Dad grinned. "I can see you really love dancing. It's written all over your face. You look so happy."

"You were so confident too," Nanna Pearl added.

"I'm very glad to hear that," Mum said.

"And I had a good appointment," Amber said, grinning. "So … thanks, Mum."

Mum hugged Amber. "I'm glad to hear you say that."

"My work here might be done soon," Nanna Pearl said, winking.

"What do you mean?" I asked her.

"My mission was to stay here and to concentrate on encouraging you and Amber to be confident," Nanna Pearl said. "I knew it was in there somewhere. I can see it in you two. This is what I wanted."

"Does that mean you're leaving?" Amber asked.

"Soon, yes, but not just yet," Nanna Pearl said.

Amber bit her bottom lip. "I wish you could stay," she said.

"I've got a lot of bingo to play, and reggae to dance to," Nanna Pearl said, with a big throaty laugh. "Besides, I'm almost done."

"Step number three?" Amber asked.

"Yes, step number three," Nanna Pearl said.

"When's that happening?" I asked.

Nanna Pearl smiled. "Tomorrow. You'll have to wait and see!"

Chapter 9

The next evening, after dinner, we sat around the kitchen table: Nanna Pearl, Mum, Dad, Amber and me. Nanna Pearl put a large glass jar on the table.

"Right, I've had an idea for something that I want you to do, even when I've gone back home," Nanna Pearl said. "I want everyone to write down something that you'd like the family to do together."

"Like playing a board game?" Dad asked.

"Or like when we did the gratitude list," Amber added.

"I'd love to go to the park," I said. "We haven't been in ages."

"That's true," Mum said. She smiled at me affectionately. "I love this idea. It's a chance for us to really get to know each other. When someone is feeling a bit down, we could take a note out and do what's written on the paper."

"*Exactly*," Nanna Pearl said. "I know it hasn't been easy lately, but I think this will be a good way for you all to take some time out. So, let's all write some actions. We've got paper and pens."

"We could also guess who wrote each idea,"

I said. "I bet we'd be able to figure out who it is."

"Perfect," Mum replied. "I'm looking forward to this."

So, we all started writing down some things we'd like to do as a family. There were so many things I wanted to do. Nanna Pearl finished first and cut up her paper and added the ideas to the jar. It was like I was dancing again, but this time it was the feeling of happiness of sitting with my family. I loved concentrating on fun activities we could do together. Every now and again, I looked up and watched everyone writing. Mum smiled at me. Dad said, "I bet you've got plenty of ideas, Emmie."

"Yes, there are so many things I want us to do," I said.

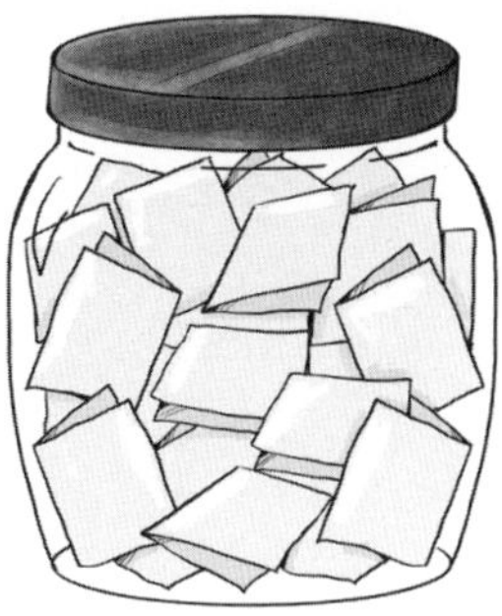

When I looked at Amber, she grinned and then made a funny face like she used to. Then I looked at Nanna Pearl.

"Almost finished?" she asked.

It had been so amazing for Nanna Pearl to be here. She'd made life exciting and now she was making sure we'd all do things together.

"Almost," I answered.

"So, does that mean you're leaving now?" Amber asked.

"Steady on, Amber," Nanna Pearl said. "I'm not ready to pack my bags just yet. I've got a ballet show to watch."

"But that won't be for a few weeks," I said.

Nanna Pearl winked. "You can't get rid of me that easily."

"Yes!" Amber and I shouted together.

Finally, we added all the slips into the jar. Dad put his hand in the jar and moved the pieces of paper around so they were all mixed up. I peered at it, wondering what we might do together.

It was a few weeks later. All the dancers from Sabrina's dance class were standing behind the curtains by the stage. The lead dancers were dressed in white leotards and skirts with ribbons, the rest of us had skirts with no ribbons and the boys were in black. Jaspreet was bouncing from one foot to the other. Leah and Alexia were sitting in the audience, ready to cheer us on.

The act before us was a group of some of the older girls. We watched closely – one day, we'd be like them! They were so strong as they moved elegantly about the stage. At the end of their performance, the audience erupted into applause.

Sabrina walked backstage to us. "Ready?" she asked. We nodded and the beginning of our music started. Jaspreet spun out onto the stage, followed by the other lead dancers. They began their routine as they'd learnt it. Soon, it was my part. Sabrina had decorated me with glitter and I'm sure it shone as I made my way onto the stage.

I ignored the bright lights and tried not to think of the large audience in front of me. I began my dance and made my way through all the steps. Soon, my part was over and we all stood in a line. We turned and stretched up towards the ceiling. The music ended, as we stood together near the edge of the stage. The audience applauded loudly and whooped.

"Well done," Sabrina said, coming out onto the stage. "I want to give a special acknowledgement to Emmie; she only started our classes a few weeks ago. Wasn't she splendid? Give a curtsey, Emmie."

I did a low curtsey and looked out into the audience as they clapped. Nanna Pearl whistled. She was going home the next day; I didn't want her to leave, but she'd told me she'd given me the tools to continue. She said she'd visit again, and she was only a phone call away if we needed her.

The Besties gathered at the end of the showcase. Me and Jaspreet had changed into tracksuits.

"You were amazing," Leah said – she looked surprised. "I want to join."

"And me," Alexia said. "And Emmie, how did you learn those steps so quickly?"

"I don't know; I loved learning, though," I said.

"Come to the class, learn it and then we can do it together," Jaspreet said. "I was so nervous."

"And me," I said.

Mum walked over with Amber. "Ready to go, Emmie?" she asked.

"Sure," I said. "See you tomorrow."

"Bye, Emmie," my friends said.

It felt like something really good had happened. I'd been worried about Amber for so long, and seen how worried Mum, Dad and Nanna Pearl had been about her. But things were changing. The dancing was the start of something too. It had given me great friends and a new interest. I knew how Amber felt now and where she'd been. Suddenly, things were looking up.

Chapter 10

"We are – " Leah shouted.

"The Besties," Jaspreet, Alexia and I shouted.

"And we want you all to join in," we shouted together.

Ms Bell came out with a large speaker. She put on the music, and Jaspreet and I did a few ballet moves. Then we all started dancing.

The other kids from our class and the other classes all looked at us for a moment. Then everyone joined in. Suddenly, we were all dancing together and twirling each other round. It had been Amber's idea to encourage everyone else to join in. We loved performing but this dance party was just as fun.

Even Ms Bell did a few moves. When the break ended, we went into the classroom. Other kids kept coming up to us and saying, “That was so cool!” and “We should do that every breaktime.” We hadn’t expected everyone to be as excited as they were.

At the end of school, we met up at Cuts & Locks. I wasn’t the only one to have new friends. Leah, Alexia and Jaspreet’s mums often came in for a cup of tea with Mum. This time, we’d asked Mum to give us all new hairstyles. Even though I didn’t like having my hair done, it would be nice to see what I looked like with a different hairstyle. I also wanted to see how my friends might look.

Mum did Jaspreet's hair, Auntie Gemma did mine and Uncle Paul did Alexia's. Nanna Pearl did Leah's hair. The other mums stood nearby, and when Nanna Pearl brought out the familiar red radio, the reggae went on and everyone started to dance.

Mum twisted Jaspreet's hair up into a knotted bun. Auntie Gemma slicked my hair back into a low bun with lots of gel. Uncle Paul did Alexia's hair in a fishtail braid, while Nanna Pearl canerowed Leah's hair.

We couldn't stop looking at our new hairstyles, and everyone took lots of photographs of our new look.

"Where's Amber?" Mum asked. "Nanna Pearl is going soon."

It felt like I had a lump in my throat that I tried to gulp down. I didn't want her to leave. "I'll see if she's at home," I said.

I made my way next door to our house and went in search of Amber. I found her in the living room. She was in the corner with her arms round her knees.

"Amber?" I asked.

She snapped her head up. Her face was wet with tears, and she wiped them away. "I don't want Nanna Pearl to go," she said, softly.

I sat next to her on the carpet and rested my head on her shoulder. "She said her job is done," I told her.

Amber laughed. I was glad to hear it; I didn't want to see her so sad.

"Aren't you going to come and say goodbye?" I asked.

"I don't know if I can," she said. "I'll miss her so much."

Nanna Pearl had followed me from the hairdresser's. She took one look at Amber and folded her into a hug. "Amber, honey," she said. "What's up?"

"I don't want you to leave," Amber said. "And I'm sure I'm not the only one. Emmie, do you want Nanna Pearl to leave?"

"No," I said. "Nanna Pearl, can't you stay?"

"This wasn't meant to be forever," Nanna Pearl said, sitting on the sofa. "Besides, I'm sure you two feel more confident now, and that's what I wanted for you. I'm so proud of you two."

I climbed onto the sofa and sat next to Nanna Pearl and Amber.

"When I write my list of what I'm grateful for, family is always at the top," Nanna Pearl said. "I'm especially thankful for my granddaughters. I'll come and visit again soon."

"It's just, what if I can't do this without you?" Amber asked. "I've never felt as comfortable with myself as I feel now, and I'm scared if you go, I won't be all right."

"I think you'll be absolutely fine," Nanna Pearl said. "I wouldn't leave otherwise. I think you're so much better and you probably haven't

even noticed how far your recovery has come."

Amber smiled.

"As for my Emerald, your dance was outstanding," Nanna Pearl said. "I want you to try and keep up your dance classes. I'm glad you have so many new friends, and I heard what The Besties did at breaktime."

"It was so much fun; everyone was dancing too," I said. "Nanna Pearl, are you sure you can't stay?"

Nanna Pearl thought for a moment. "I have some travelling to do but I will be back," she said. "And you'll be able to show me all your new dances. Remember what I told you – it's OK to be different!"

"I know everyone looks different," I said. "But I share lots of the same interests as my friends. We all look different in our own way and that's OK."

"That's exactly right, and you, Amber?" Nanna Pearl asked.

"I am different," Amber said, thoughtfully, "but I don't see it as a bad thing any more."

"That's great to hear," Nanna Pearl said. "Come on, it's time for me to go."

Amber and I quickly got changed and made our way back to the hairdresser's. Dad put Nanna Pearl's suitcases in the boot of the car and then climbed in the front seat.

Mum hugged Nanna Pearl closely and gave her a snack for the journey. Nanna Pearl laughed at this and then she hugged all of us again.

"I'll come and visit again soon," Nanna Pearl

said. "Keep up everything I taught you, OK?"

We nodded.

"Thank you," Mum said. "You've really helped us work together as a family."

"It was my pleasure," Nanna Pearl said. "I've really enjoyed being here. Bye, everyone."

Nanna Pearl waved at us and climbed into the car. Her earrings jangled as she climbed inside. The Besties crowded around me, and we all stood on the street as the car pulled away from the house and drove off down the street.

"Come on," Leah said. "We need to think of a new routine for after half term."

"Sure," I said. "Can Amber help make one?"

The other girls nodded. Amber followed us inside and we prepared to make up a new dance. I looked around at my new friends and thought about the lessons Nanna Pearl had taught me. We were all different in our own way, but I realised this just made us all stronger.

CUTS & LOCKS

Nanna Pearl's feel-good moves!

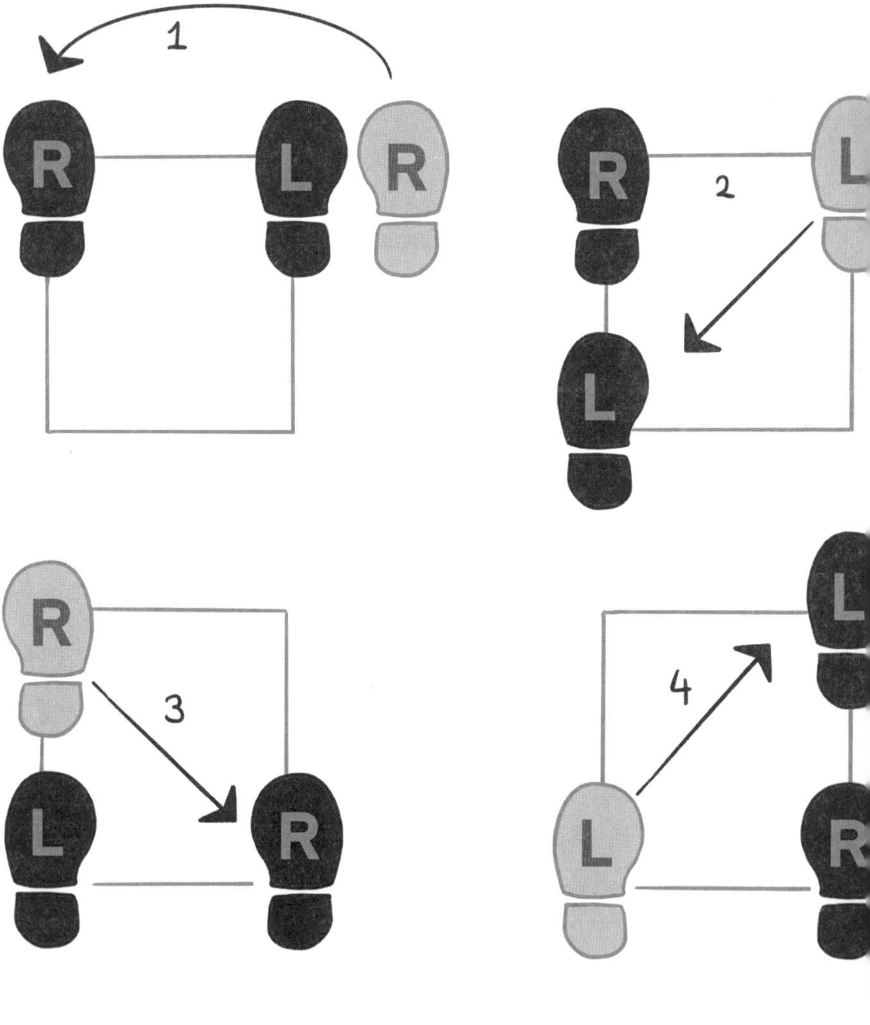

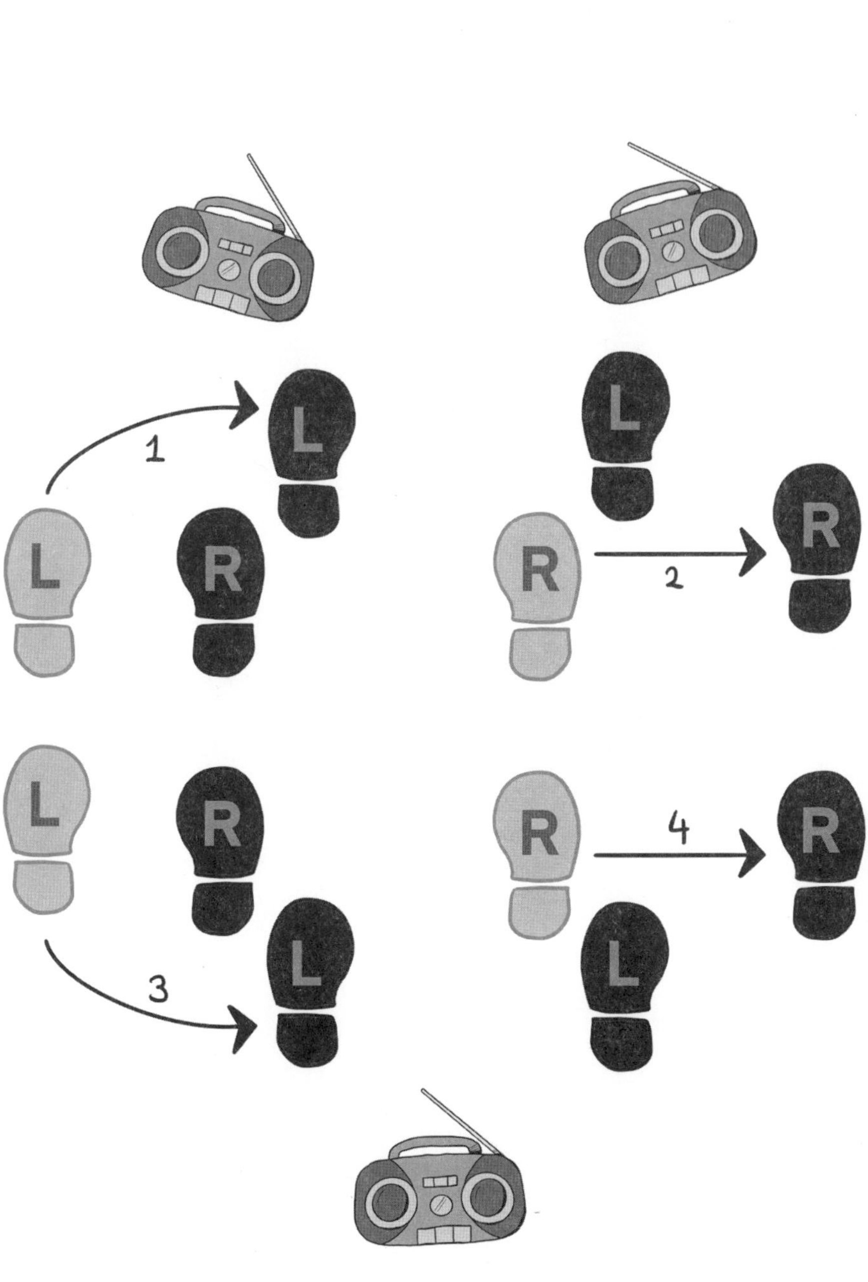
L
1
L
R
L
2
R
R
L
R
L
3
R
4
R
L

Book talk questions

How does Emmie's relationship with her Nanna Pearl help her grow in the story?

Why does Emmie struggle with her self-image, and how does that change over the course of the book?

What role does dance and reggae music play in Emmie's self-discovery?

How do your friends support you?

What does the book say about family support and the importance of role models?

How does Emmie learn to embrace her uniqueness by the end of the story?

Did you relate to any of the characters in the story?

Why do you think that Emmie joining the ballet class is important?

How does Nanna Pearl's influence shape Emmie's perspective on life?

What do you think Emmie's journey teaches about embracing differences and finding beauty in ourselves?

Ask the author

How did you start writing?

As a young child in primary school, I was always writing stories which mainly focused on fantasy worlds. When I was eleven, my teacher said he thought I could be an author and from then I took my writing seriously.

What inspired you to write about self-love and body positivity?

Body image is something I struggled with when I was younger and it's only now that I'm focusing on my own self-love and learning to appreciate my body. We're all different and it's easy to compare yourself with others but I love that we're all unique. I wanted to share this thinking with those who might feel the same.

What was the inspiration behind Nanna Pearl's character?

Nanna Pearl is a mixture of my mum and Auntie Rose. They are very strong women who always have time for their families and me. They have helped me grow as a person and I can always talk to them when I have an issue. I really wanted Emmie to have that as she discovers more about herself.

How do you hope Emmie's journey influences readers who might feel out of place?

I hope readers understand that we are all different. I hope Emmie's journey shows ways that we can learn to love ourselves and also appreciate those around us. I hope her journey encourages readers to speak to their loved ones about how they're feeling.

Why did you choose reggae music as a central theme in the story?

My mum would play reggae when I was younger, and it is a type of music that I love. My heritage is Jamaican, and the music comes from there. However, it is the kind of sound that can unite people no matter where they come from as it is so upbeat and entertaining. I wanted to use music that can join the family together and that Emmie could explore with Nanna Pearl.

Collins BIG CAT

Published by Collins
An imprint of HarperCollins*Publishers*

The News Building
1 London Bridge Street
London SE1 9GF
UK

Macken House
39/40 Mayor Street Upper
Dublin 1
D01 C9W8
Ireland

10 9 8 7 6 5 4 3 2 1

ISBN 978-0-00-874477-9

British Library Cataloguing-in-Publication Data
A catalogue record for this publication is available from the British Library.

Author: Kimberly Redway
Illustrator: Afua Bedlako (Beehive Illustration)
Publisher: Laura White
Commissioning editor: Holly Woolnough
Development editor: Zoë Clarke
Product manager: Holly Woolnough
Content editor: Selin Akca
Copyeditor: Sally Byford
Proofreader: Catherine Dakin
Reviewer: Lisa Davis
Cover designer: Sarah Finan
Internal design: 2Hoots Publishing Services Ltd
Typesetter: Jouve India Ltd
Production controller: Katharine Willard

Collins would like to thank the teachers and children at Grange Primary School, Southwark, for being part of the development of Big Cat Read On.

With thanks to Beat for their help reviewing this book.

Printed in the UK

FSC www.fsc.org MIX Paper | Supporting responsible forestry FSC™ C007454

This book contains FSC™ certified paper and other controlled sources to ensure responsible forest management.

For more information visit: www.harpercollins.co.uk/green

Made with responsibly sourced paper and vegetable ink

Scan to see how we are reducing our environmental impact.